HISTOIRE DU SOLDAT
AND
RENARD

IN FULL SCORE

Igor Stravinsky

DOVER PUBLICATIONS, INC.
New York

Bibliographical Note

This Dover edition, first published in 1995, is a new compilation of two scores originally published separately. *Renard: Histoire burlesque chantée et jouée* (this title also appears in Russian and German) was originally published by Ad. Henn/J. & W. Chester, Ltd. (Chester Music), London, 1917. *Histoire du Soldat* (this title also appears in German and English) was originally published in an unidentified authoritative edition, n.d. The Dover edition adds: new lists of contents and instrumentation, expanded; a glossary of French terms in both scores, including translations of footnotes; and prefatory notes for both works. Minor corrections have been made throughout.

Library of Congress Cataloging-in-Publication Data

Stravinsky, Igor, 1882–1971.
    [Histoire du soldat. Polyglot]
    Histoire du soldat ; and, Renard / Igor Stravinsky.—In full score.
    1 score.
    Histoire du soldat, for narrator, 3 actors, and septet (clarinet, bassoon, cornet, trombone, violin, double bass, and percussion); French libretto by Charles-Ferdinand Ramuz; English, French, and German words.
    Renard, a burlesque in song and dance in 1 act for clowns, dancers, and acrobats with large chamber ensemble and 4 men's voices; Russian text by the composer, adapted from Russian folktales; French singing version by Charles-Ferdinand Ramuz; French, German, and Russian words.
    ISBN 0-486-28525-1
    1. Ballets—Scores. I. Ramuz, C. F. (Charles Ferdinand), 1878–1947.
II. Stravinsky, Igor, 1882–1971. Baika. Polyglot. III. Title.
M1520.S9H415 1995   95-198
                                                            CIP
                                                             M

Manufactured in the United States of America
Dover Publications, Inc., 31 East 2nd Street, Mineola, N.Y. 11501

Contents

Glossary of French Terms

Translations of footnotes and longer score notes appear at the end of this section.

à grelots, with jingles [tambourine]
à pointe, at the tip [of the bow]
au bord, at the edge [of the drum head]
au milieu, in the middle [of the drum head]
au talon, at the heel [of the bow]
avec grelots, with jingles [tambourine]
avec le pouce, thumb roll [tambourine]

bag (uette), stick, beater [percussion]
    à tete en capoc [kapok], with a medium-soft cushioned head
    en bois, wooden snare drum stick
    en cuir, with a hide-covered head
    en éponge, with a soft ("sponge") head
    en feutre (dur), with a (hard) felt-covered head
    en jonc, with a stiff cane shaft
bois, wood (shaft of a beater); *les bois*, woodwinds
bouché, "stopped" sound [horn]

comme plus haut, as above
coup de genou(x), struck on the knee(s) [tambourine]
court, short
cuivré, brassy
cuivrez, play with a resounding sound

de la m(ain) d(roite), with the right hand
de la m(ain) g(auche), with the left hand
de la membrane, of the drumhead
du milieu de l'archet, from the middle of the bow
du talon, from the heel [of the bow]

enchaînez, segue
en dehors, distant
en glissant le doigt, while sliding the finger
en harmoniques, in harmonics [strings]
environ, approximately [tempo]
et, and
étouffez, "choked" [cut-off sound]

fin(e), end

gliss(ando) pour la timb(ale) à levier, *glissando* for the pedal timpani
grand(e), large
grand détaché, bowing with broad, separate motions
grande taille, large size [drum]

jeté, bounced, "thrown" bowing
jusqu'au même signe X, until the same sign X

laissez vibrer, let it sound

mailloche, bass drum beater
m(ain) d(roite), right hand
m(ain) g(auche), left hand
manière d'exécution, playing method

non cuivré, not brassy

petit(e), small
petite taille, small size [drum]
préparez la sourdine, have the mute ready
préparez vite, quickly prepare
près du chevalet, near the bridge [cimbalom]

reprendre l'archet, pick up the bow

sans grelots, without jingles [tambourine]
sans timbre, without snares [drum]
sec, dry, abrupt
sur (la corde) Ré [Do, Sol, etc.], on the D [C, G, etc.] string
sur la touche, on the fingerboard [of the violin, etc.]

talon, heel [of the bow]
tout l'archet, full bow
très court, very short
très en dehors, very distant
très sec, very dry, abrupt
très serré, very tight, compact [string tremolo]

un peu velouté, a bit velvety

Footnotes and Longer Score Notes

In *Renard:*

Page 10, footnote (for Cimbalom):
Les notes marqués du signe "o" se jouent derrière le chevalet de l'instrument
The notes marked "o" are to be played behind the bridge of the instrument

Page 28, footnote (for Tenor II):
Prononcez: confessère
Pronounce [confesser]: confessère

Page 41, footnote (for Cimbalom):
Pour l'instrument qui a le ré grave exécuter . . .
For an instrument with the low D, play . . .
[Similar footnotes appear on pp. 42, 43, 61, 92, 93, 94, 110 and 111.]

Page 55, footnote (for Tenor I):
Note basse indeterminée
Indefinite low pitch

Page 57, 2nd bar, Cimbalom:
ouvrez peu à peu la pédale
open [depress] the pedal little by little
[reoccurs on p. 75, 1st bar]

Page 78, footnotes (for Bass I, Tenor I):
[For the Russian text, sing the phrase as shown.]
Pour le français et l'allemand cette fin de la phrase est confiée au 1er ténor, la basse se taisant.
For the French and German texts, this phrase ending is for Tenor I only, Bass I remaining silent.

Page 105, footnote (for Cimbalom, Cello, Bass and Timpani):
Pour l'instrument qui a le ré grave, exécuter . . .
Supprimez dans ce cas les parties des Violoncelle, Contrabasse et timbales du 63
For [a cimbalom] with the low D, play . . . [*example*]
In this case, omit the cello, bass and timpani parts from 63
[continues through pp. 106–7, then again at p. 115]

Page 112, footnote (for Cimbalom and Timpani):
En cas que le ré grave du Cimbalum [sic] *manque remplacez-le par la timbale*
If the cimbalom's low D is missing, let the timpani play that note.
[continues through pp. 113–114]

Page 123, footnote (for Bass I):
The Russian note says: "The transition from the *yeh*-sound to the *oo*-sound should be sudden. The *oo*-sound should be pronounced with the lips, imitating the sound of the lowest string on the bass."
[reoccurs on p. 127]

Page 132, footnote (for Cimbalom and Bass):
Ces notes mises entre parenthèse se jouent seulement au cas où le Cimbalum ne possède pas le ré grave.
Play the parenthetical notes [in the bass part] only if the cimbalom lacks a low D.
[continues through pp. 133, 137, 140, 141, 146, 147 and 151]

In *Histoire du Soldat:*

Page 166, footnote (for Percussion):
Tenir dans la main droite une baguette en jonc à tête en capoc et se servir de celle-ci pour frapper le tambour de basque et la caisse claire; dans la main gauche—la mailloche pour frapper la grosse caisse
The right hand holds a beater with a stiff cane shaft and a medium-soft cushioned head; this is used to strike the tambourine and the side [snare] drum. A bass drum beater in the left hand strikes the bass drum.
[Similar footnotes appear on pp. 167, 176 and (expanded) 201.]

Page 181, 1st bar, Cornet:
mais moins fort que les bois
but softer than the woodwinds
[reoccurs on p. 188 at Fig. 16 and p. 191 at Fig. 20]

Page 181, after Fig. 1, Percussion:
au bord [et] au milieu . . . de la membrane
at the edge and at the middle of the drumhead
[reoccurs on p. 186 (footnote), p. 188 after Fig. 15 and p. 196 (footnote)]

Page 195, before Fig. 14, Violin:
glissez avec l'archet de toute sa longueur
slide [play this passage] with full bows
[reoccurs on p. 202 at Fig. 4 (". . . until the sign X") and on p. 204 at Fig. 8 and after Fig. 9]

Page 201, footnote (for Percussion):
Remarque générale pour la percussion du TANGO: *L'exécutant tient la mailloche (de la Gr. C.) dans sa main gauche et dans sa main droite une baguette à tête de capoc (avec le manche en jonc). Les notes avec les queues en haut appartiennent à la main droite (c. à. d. [c'est à dire] à la baguette en capoc), celles avec les queues en bas, à la main gauche (c. à. d. à la mailloche). La cymbale (fixée à la Gr. C.) est légèrement frappée au bord, seulement par le manche en jonc de la baguette en capoc. Pour la disposition des tambours consultez la page consacrée à la disposition de l'orchestre.*
General remark about percussion in the TANGO: The player holds the bass drum beater in his left hand and, in his right, a beater with a stiff cane shaft and a

medium-soft cushioned head. The upstemmed notes belong to the right hand (that is, to the cushioned-head beater); the downstemmed notes, to the left hand (the bass drum beater). The cymbal attached to the bass drum is struck lightly on its edge, and only with the cane shaft. For the setup of the drums, see the instrumentation page.

Page 202, footnote (for the Violin instructions at Fig. 4):
Exception faite des endroits marqués par le "saltando"
Except for passages marked "saltando"
[reoccurs on p. 204 between Fig. 8 and the end of the section]

Page 208, footnote (for Percussion):
Toute cette percussion est (légèrement) frappée avec la tringle du triangle. Le triangle est tenu de la main gauche de l'exécutant; à sa droite, se trouvent (très près) l'un en face de l'autre, la C. cl. et le Tamb. de basque (posés de champ, ce qui est plus commode pour l'exécutant); à sa gauche la Grosse caisse.
All percussion are lightly struck with the triangle beater [metal rod]. The player holds the triangle in his left hand; close to his right, and next to one another, are the side [snare] drum and the tambourine (resting on their side for easier playing); the bass drum is to the player's left.

Page 211, footnote (for Percussion):
°La Gr. C. se trouve à gauche et les 2 C. cl. juste en face de l'exécutant, et très près l'une de l'autre. Frappez ces instruments avec une baguette à tête en capoc que l'exécutant tient dans sa main gauche. Dans sa main droite il tient une baguette mince à petite tête en éponge (qu'il lui faudrait tenir prête pour le No. $\boxed{34}$).

The bass drum is placed to the player's left; the two side [snare] drums, very close to each other, are in front of the player. These [three] instruments are struck with a cushioned-head beater held in his left hand. In his right, to prepare for the passage at $\boxed{34}$, he holds a thin beater with a small sponge head.

°°Exécuter avec la bag. à tête d'éponge dont l'exécutant prendra soin de tenir la tête tournée en bas et de la manier rien qu'avec les doigts (le bras restant parfaitemente immobile) de façon à donner au rythme une allure mécanique et précise.
[This passage] is played with the sponge-headed beater carefully held head down and controlled solely by the fingers (the arm remains motionless) in order to give the rhythm a precise, machine-like drive.

Page 213, footnote (for Percussion):
Placez ces deux instruments de champ, très près l'un de l'autre de façon à pouvoir manier aisément la baguette (m. dr.) entre leurs membranes dans le mouvement indiqué.
Place these two instruments on their side, very close to each other, so that the beater (in the right hand) can be easily manipulated between the two drumheads in the given rhythm.

Page 224, 1st bar, Percussion:
Les queues en haut pour la m.d., les queues en bas pour la main gauche.
The right hand plays the upstemmed notes; the left hand, the downstemmed notes.
[reoccurs on p. 227 at Fig. 8]

RENARD
[The Fox, 1915–16]

A burlesque in song and dance
in one act

For clowns, dancers and acrobats
With large chamber ensemble and four men's voices

Почтительнѣйше посвящается
Княгинѣ
Е. де Полиньякъ

Très respectueusement dédié
à Madame la Princesse
Edmond de Polignac

Note

The chamber opera *Renard* was commissioned by the Princess Edmond de Polignac, whose Parisian salon Stravinsky had attended, and the work is dedicated to her. It is one of the intensely Russian pieces written during the composer's wartime sojourn in the French-speaking area of Switzerland, 1914–1920. It was composed in the years 1915 and 1916, but not performed until 1922, when it was produced by Diaghilev in Paris to designs by Mikhail Larionov. The composer later told interviewers that he had made no conscious use of authentic folk melodies.

Stravinsky intended the characters' roles to be performed in mime by clowns, dancers and acrobats, all of whom remain constantly on stage between the entrance and exit marches. The vocalists, two tenors and two basses, were meant to sit in the small orchestra, which included a Hungarian cimbalom that Stravinsky had discovered and purchased in a Geneva café. The orchestra was to sit behind the dancers, sharing their podium, unless the performance was in a theater, in which case the dancing was to be done in front of the curtain. (In Larionov's design, the characters wore animal masks that sat atop their heads and did not cover the full face; the Rooster's tree was a simple platform on a post with a ladder reaching to the stage floor.) The four voices are generally not linked to specific characters, although in the dialogues between the Rooster and the Fox, the Rooster's lines are frequently assigned to Tenor I, the fox's to Tenor II.

The Russian text (the original one) was written by Stravinsky himself, who adapted folktales from the famous collection by Afanasiev, the Russian "Grimm." The verbal and conceptual world is that of the old peasantry and the language is quite specialized, including folklike diminutives, colloquial word forms, regional vocabulary and liturgical Old Church Slavonic forms (in the Fox's role as a nun). Furthermore, words are distorted for comic effect, and are often there more for their sound than for their sense: for instance, the opening fivefold *Kudá?* ("Where to?"—presumably with the connotation "Where has he gotten to?") resembles a rooster's call. The Russian title is *Báǐka,* meaning "a narrative."

The French version, by the composer's new Swiss friend Charles-Ferdinand Ramuz, a distinguished regional novelist who also worked with Stravinsky on *Histoire du soldat* and other projects, was based on a word-for-word French translation provided by the composer, but the final result is not, and never was, intended as a literal or even close translation. Instead, it is an independent singing version, less concerned with preserving the meaning than with fitting the music exactly and with (largely) respecting the original rhyme scheme and even the original vowel coloring: note that the first words of the French, the fivefold "Où ça?" ("Where?") have the same vowel sounds as *Kudá?* As far as the meaning is concerned, the French occasionally translates the Russian, but much more often is an extremely free adaptation that is equally suitable to the action that is taking place. (The German text in the present volume, by Rupert Koller, often hews closely to the French, but also goes its own way much of the time.)

For many of the above considerations, and because words are frequently repeated, either exactly or with slight variations, it is not feasible to offer a complete exact translation of the original Russian text in libretto form. What follows, instead, is a tight, detailed synopsis of the Russian, with references to the pages of the score.

Renard: A Synopsis

The dancers enter to a march (pp. 7–9). The Rooster calls for the capture of a hated person whom he wants to trample, split with an axe, stab and hang (pp. 10–23). "I sit in the oak tree," he continues, "I guard the house and I sing a song" (pp. 24–25). The Fox (a female character) arrives disguised as a nun and urges the Rooster to come down and make confession, saying she has come, hungry and thirsty, from a distant wilderness for that purpose (pp. 25–28). The Rooster recognizes the Fox and says sarcastically that he hasn't fasted or prayed, so: "Come another time" (p. 29). The Fox/Nun accuses the Rooster of having evil thoughts and too many wives; some men have ten, twenty or forty and, whenever they meet, fight over their wives as if over concubines; the Rooster should come down and not die in sin (pp. 30–37). The Rooster leaps to the ground and is seized by the Fox, who drags him around the stage; the Rooster laments that he is being carried off over rugged terrain to the ends of the earth (pp. 37–40).

The Rooster calls on the Cat and the Ram for aid (pp. 41–44). They appear and ask the Fox if she isn't going to share her easily gained catch, since they are hungry and aggressive (pp. 45–49). The Fox releases the Rooster and runs off; the Rooster, Cat and Ram dance (p. 50). They mock the Fox's boastfulness, and sing of how the Rooster left the barnyard with his hens and was greeted by the Fox, who expected a meal, how the Rooster begged not to be eaten and offered the hens instead; the Fox wanted the Rooster only, grabbed him and carried him far off, the Rooster shrieked for help but the hens didn't hear (pp. 51–70). The Cat and the Ram depart and the Rooster regains his perch (pp. 70–71).

The Fox returns, casts off her nun's robe and, complimenting the Rooster on his appearance, asks him to look out the window and receive peas as a reward; the Rooster refuses, saying he prefers cereal; the Fox then says she has a big house full of wheat; the Rooster says he's full; the Fox offers a pancake, the Rooster isn't fooled; again the Fox asks the Rooster to descend so she can carry his soul up to heaven (pp. 71–87). The Rooster prepares to jump down, and the First Tenor shouts, "Fox, don't eat meat on a fast day"; the Rooster jumps, the Fox seizes him, and the Second Tenor says: "It may be forbidden to some, but it's all right for us!" (p. 87). The Rooster makes the same lament as

3

before, and appeals to the Cat and Ram as before (pp. 88–94). The Fox carries the Rooster off to one side and starts to pluck him; the Rooster says that the Fox is expected for dinner at the home of the Rooster's father, where buttered *blinis, pirogi* and porridge await her; he then asks the Lord to remember and preserve all his relatives, naming them individually (pp. 95–104).

Just as the Rooster is passing out, the Cat and Ram appear and, to the accompaniment of a *gusli* (psaltery), they sing a soothing song: "Is Ivanova the Fox at home in her golden lair with her little children?"; they name the Fox's daughters (pp. 104–116). The Fox sticks the tip of her nose out of her earth and asks who is calling her; they say that animals are coming with a scythe [they themselves have one!] to cut her up, that they have watched so that the animals didn't eat her up, and that they have run to prevent the animals from tearing her apart, etc.; then they catch her by the tail, drag her out by it and throttle her (pp. 117–131). The Rooster, Cat and Ram dance and sing in mockery of the Fox's unexpected death; most of the song text is an untranslatable farrago of folk sayings barely related to the plot (pp. 132–152). The dancers exit to a reprise of the opening march (pp. 153–154).

STANLEY APPELBAUM

4

Instrumentation

° ⎡ Piccolo [Fl. picc.]
  ⎣ Flute [Flauto grande, Fl. gr.]

° ⎡ Oboe [Ob.]
  ⎣ English Horn [Corno inglese, Cor. ingl.]

° ⎡ Clarinet in E♭ [Clarinetto piccolo, Cl. picc. (Mi♭)]
  ⎣ Clarinet in A, B♭ [Cl. (La, Si♭)]

Bassoon [Fagotto, Fg.]

2 Horns in F [Corni, Cor. (Fa)]
Trumpet in A, B♭ [Tromba, Tr. (La, Si♭)]

Cimbalom°° [Cimb. hungar., Cimb.]

Timpani (Pedal) [Timp., Timb(ale) à levier]

Percussion:
    Tambourine with jingles [T.d.B. (Tambour de Basque) à grelots]
    Tambourine without jingles [T.d.B. sans grelots]
    Small Side Drum [Caisse claire, C. cl., C. c. P.]
    Triangle [Triangolo, Trgl.]
    Cymbals [Piatti(e), Ptti.]
    Bass Drum [Gran cassa, Gr. c.]

(For a list of percussion beaters, see the Glossary, p. v, under *baguette*.)

Singers:
    2 Solo Tenors [Tenori I, II]
    2 Solo Basses [Bassi I, II]

Solo Strings:
    Violin I [Violino I, Vl.]
    Violin II [Violino II, Vl.]
    Viola [Viola, Vla.]
    Cello [Violoncello, Vlc.]
    Bass [Contrabasso, Cb.]

°one player

°°The cimbalom, a type of dulcimer traditionally found in the Magyar orchestra, is played by striking its array of open strings with small beaters. The sound varies according to the kind of "stick" (*baguette*)—either leather-tipped (*en cuir*) or wooden-tipped (*en bois*)—and its placement on the string: in the center or near the bridge (*près du chevalet*). Some modern instruments have a damper pedal, permitting an increasingly resonant sound (*ouvrez peu à peu la Pédale*), or a resounding sound (*cuivrez*). Although the cimbalom's complete chromatic compass extends from E below the bass staff to the E four octaves higher, Stravinsky's score provides alternate passages for an instrument with a low D (*pour l'instrument qui possède le ré grave*).

MARCHE [MARCH]

Entrance of the Actors

*) Les notes marqués du signe „o" se jouent derrière le chevalet de l'instrument

25
Cimb.
f
T. I
Куда, куда, куда, куда, ку-
Où ça, où ça, où ça où
Oh Gott, oh Gott, oh Gott, was
B. II
-га ми стопчу, И то-(о) по-ромъ срублю.
cass'-ra les os, on vous lui plan-t'ra le cou-teau
Kno-chen bre-chen, wol-len ihn__ ab-ste-chen.
Vl. I
Vl. II
Vla.
Vlc.
Cb.
25

ду - бу, Си жу,домъстере-гу, _____ Пѣ сню по-ю.
mon bâ-ton, je garde la mai-son, _____ j'chant'ma chanson.
War-te aus, sing ich in al - le Welt _____ ich wahr'dies Haus.

70

Cor. ingl. = Oboe

(Приходитъ лиса въ одѣянiи монахини.)
(Arrive Renard en costume de religieuse)
(Der Fuchs kommt als Mönch verkleidet)

(Лиса продолжаетъ)
(Renard continuant)
(Der Fuchs fährt fort)

Мно-го ну-жды пре-тер пѣ-(ѣ)ла; Те - бя, ми-ло-е ча - до!
Ai, souf-fert beaucoup d'mi-sèr's; j'suis i-ci, fils très cher, a
Ohn' Speis' und Trank,von We-ges Müh'n krank,komm ich die See-le dein, be-

Спо-вѣ - -дать хо-тѣ-(ѣ)-ла.
fin d'vous con - fes - ser*)
wah - ren vor ew'-ger Not und_ Pein._

*) Prononcez: confessère

сой - дё - тесь, тутъ и де - рё-тесь О сво-ихъ же-нахъ,
où vous vous ren-con - trez, vous vous bat - tez, rap - port à vos fem mes,
auch_ bei-sam-men seid, habt ihr um eu - re Eh'frau'n Streit, wie um

18 colla parte

какъ о на - ло - (о) - (о)-жницахъ. Сни - ди, ми - ло - е
comm' si c'é - taient vos maî - tress's; viens mon fils, jusqu'à
käuf-li-che Frau'ns-per - so - nen. Denk auch, mein lie - ber Sohn,

18 colla parte

120

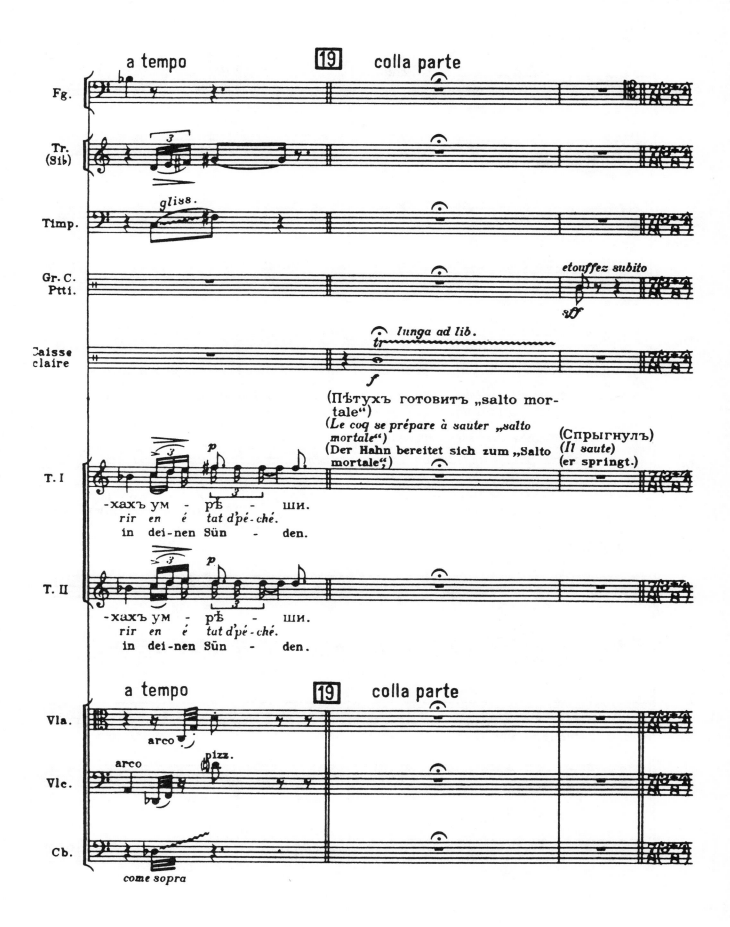

20 Stringendo (♩.= 126)
130
Fl. gr.
f
Fg.
mf
f
Cimb.
f
sempre poco sf
Timp.
(Лиса схвативаетъ пѣтуха и носится съ нимъ по сценѣ, держа его подмышкой)
(Renard saisit le coq et tourne autour de la scène en le tenant sous le bras)
(Der Fuchs stürzt sich auf den Hahn, ergreift ihn unter den Achseln und schleppt ihn über die Szene)
(Пѣтухъ отчаянно отбивается)
(Le coq se débattant désespérément)
(Der Hahn wehrt sich verzweifelt)
T. I
По - не - сла ме - ня ли - са, По - не - сла пѣ - ту -
Ah! mon Dieu! mon Dieu! mon Dieu! Il me tir' par la
Oh, mein Gott, o du mein Gott, hilf doch, er macht mich
20 Stringendo (♩.= 126)
(pizz.)
Vl. I
f
(pizz.)
Vl. II
f
Vla.
stacc. e sempre sff
Vlc.
arco, stacc. e sff sempre
Cb.
arco, stacc. e sff sempre
130

Fl. gr.
Fg.
come sopra
Cimb.
Timp.
T. I
-ха, По-кру-тымъ бе-реж - -камъ, По вы - со-кимъ го -
queue... Il me tir' par la queue, il dé - chir' mes ha -
tot, er zerrt mich, zer-beißt mich, er zer - fetzt und zer -
Vl. I
Vl. II
Vla.
Vlc.
Cb.
21
Fl. gr.
Fg.
Tr. (Si♭)
(sord.)
sf
Cimb.
Timp.
T. I
-рамъ, Въчу-жі-я зе - мли, Въ да-ле-кі-я стра-ны,
bits, il me lâch' - ra plus Qu'à trent' six lieues d'i - ci,
reißt mich, mein schö-nes Kleid, mein schö-nes Fe - der-kleid,
Vl. II

За три де - вять зе - мель, Въ тридца - то - е царст во, Въ три-де-
(trois et trois qui font six, et trois fois trois qui font dix, et trois
und verschleppt mich so weit, so weit — von hier, hat denn kei - ner

135

- ся - - то - е го - су - дарст - во;
fois dix et six trent six!)
Mit - leid, Mit - leid mit mir?

Котъ да ба ранъ, Хо четъсъѣстьме-ня ли - ca!
Frèr' bouc, frèr' chut, c'gros glou-ton me mang'-ra,
Barm - her - zig - keit! Böck-chen, Ka - ter-chen, Brü-der-lein,

*) Pour l'instrument qui a le ré grave exécuter:
Das Instrument, welches das tiefe d hat, spielt:

Котъ да ба ранъ,   Хо четъ съѣсть пѣ ту - ха!
frèr' bouc, frèr' chat,   *bons a mis, e - cou - tez moi,*
Barm - her - zig - keit!   **E - wig will ich euch dank-bar sein**

*) come sopra

*) come sopra

Cl. in Sib = Cl. picc. in Mib

46   RENARD

Не куп - лен-но - е у____ те - бя, де - ше - во - е;
c'que tu   as dans l'bec____   ne   t'a pas   coû-té   cher,
hat   sich bil - lig   was recht Gu - tes   er-gat - tert;

(Лиса выпускаетъ пѣтуха и быстро убѣгаетъ. Пѣтухъ, котъ да баранъ пляшутъ)
(Renard lâche le coq et s'en fuit. Le coq, le chat et le bouc dansent)
(Der Fuchs läßt den Hahn los und entflieht. Hahn, Kater und Bock tanzen einen Freudentanz)

170

*) Неопредѣленно низкая нота
Note basse indeterminée

*) En cas d'absence du *Ré* grave / Falls das tiefe *D* fehlt
**) parlando (*mezza voce*)

Хо - чу пѣ -ту - ши - на - го!"
J'au - rai ta peau, j'au - rai tes os!"
such' mir ein Hähn-chen zum Ri-sot-to."

*) Исполнять такъ:

сыт-(та) не-хо - чу.

**) *Pour le française et l'allemand cette fin de la phrase est confiée au 1er tenor, la basse se taisant.*

**) Im Französischen und Deutschen wird das Ende des Satzes vom 1. Tenor gesungen, während der Baß pausiert.

Ку - куа-ре-ку пѣ-ту-шокъ,   Зо - ло-той гре-бе-шокъ,
Co - co - ri - co, sei - gneur coq,   Crêt' d'Or Têt'-bien-coif-fée
Ki - ke-ri - ki lie-ber Hahn!   Bist so schön an-ge-tan,

305

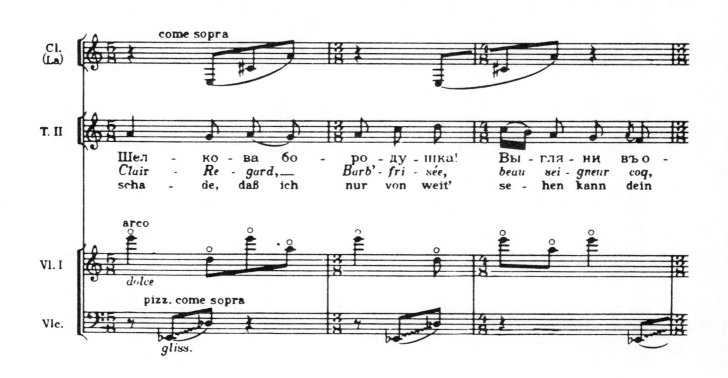

Шел - ко-ва бо - ро-душка!   Вы-гля-ни въ о-
Clair - Re - gard,___   Barb'-fri-sée,   beau sei-gneur coq,
scha - de, daß ich   nur von weit'   se-hen kann dein

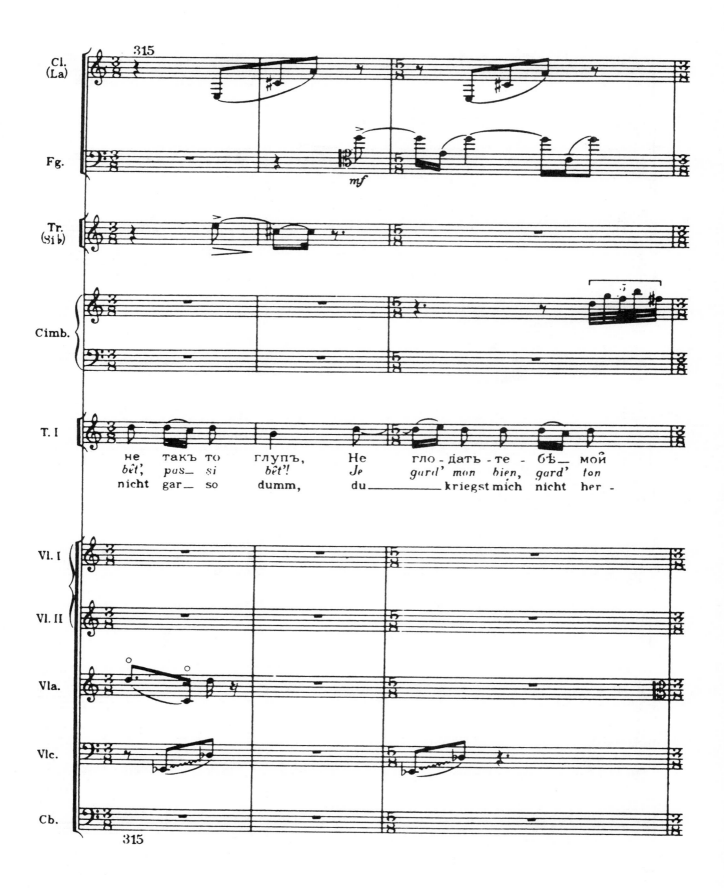

не такъ то глупъ, Не гло - дать те - бѣ мой
bêt', pas si bêt'! Je gard' mon bien, gard' ton
nicht gar so dumm, du kriegst mich nicht her -

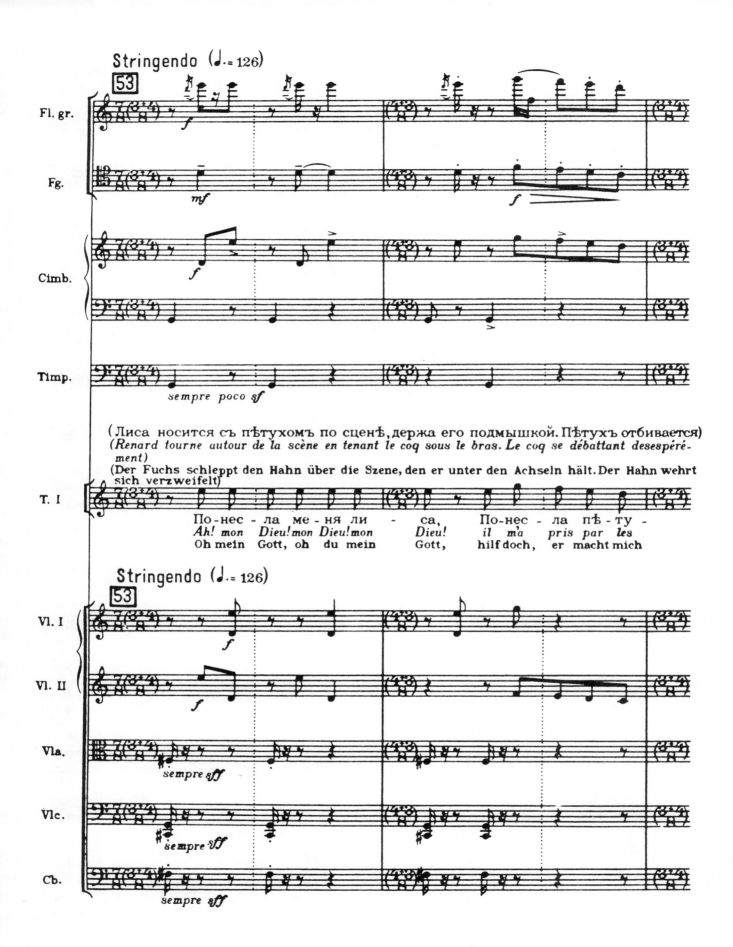

(Лиса носится съ пѣтухомъ по сценѣ, держа его подмышкой. Пѣтухъ отбивается)
(Renard tourne autour de la scène en tenant le coq sous le bras. Le coq se débattant desespérément)
(Der Fuchs schleppt den Hahn über die Szene, den er unter den Achseln hält. Der Hahn wehrt sich verzweifelt)

По-нес - ла ме - ня ли - са,   По-нес - ла пѣ-ту-
Ah! mon Dieu! mon Dieu! mon   Dieu!   il m'a   pris par les
Oh mein Gott, oh du mein   Gott,   hilf doch,   er macht mich

345

*) Pour l'instrument qui possède le ré grave exécuter:
   Das Instrument mit dem tiefen d spielt:

350

Fl. gr.

Ob.

Cl. (La)

Fg.

Cor. (Fa)

Tr. (Sib)

Cimb.

Timp.

T. I

Котъ да ба ранъ, Хо четъ съѣсть пѣ ту ха!
frèr' bouc, frèr chat, bons a - mis, e - cou - tez moi,
Barm - her - zig - keit, e - wig will ich euch dankbar sein,

Vl. I

arco   pizz.   arco   pizz.

Vl. II

arco   pizz.   arco   pizz.

Vla.

arco   pizz.   arco   pizz.

Vlc.

Cb.

350

*) come sopra

По - мя - ни, Гос-по-ди Си - - до - ра, Ма -
Sei - gneur, prends sous ta gard' Sé - - ra - phi - ne,
Herr Gott, er - barm'dich, er - hö - re mich, laß

-ка - ра, Треть-я - го За - ха - ра,Трехъ Ма-
ma cou-sin', ma ——— bonn' mar-rain' Cath'rine, tous les
dei - ner Huld emp-foh - len sein mein Müt - ter -

*) Pour l'instrument qui a le RÉ grave, exécuter:
Supprimez dans ce cas les parties des Violoncelle, Contrebasse et tim-
bales du 63
Das Instrument mit dem tiefen d spielt:
In diesem Fall pausieren Violoncello, Kontrabaß und Pauken bei 63

405

Да со сво - и - ми ма - лы - ми дѣ - ту - шка - ми?
Pour rait on____ par - ler à ses d'moi - sell's
Von ihm selbst o - der sei - nem Töch - ter - lein.

дѣ, Да со сво - и - ми ма - лы - ми дѣ - ту - шка - ми?
ler? Pour rait on____ par - ler à ses d'moi - sell's
sein, von ihm selbst o - der sei - nem Töch - ter - lein.

mf
415

Тюкъ,тюкъ, гу - сельцы, ба - ра - но - вы стру - ноч - ки... Тюкъ,тюкъ...
Tiouc, tiouc, on vouschante tout doux,pour l'a - mour de vous... Tiouc, tiouc...
Pink, Pink, sach-te Saitchen,kling',daß unsder schlaue Plan ge-lingt.Pink, Pink.

420

*) pour l'instrument qui a le RÉ grave
   für das Instrument, welches das tiefe D hat

*) En cas que le Ré grave du Cimbalum manque remplacez le par la timbale
Wenn das Cimbalum kein tiefes D hat, soll es durch die Pauke ersetzt werden

Тюкъ, тюкъ,
Tiouc, tiouc...
Pink, Pink,

А   чет-вер-та - я   Зажми - ку - ла-чекъ.
et .   la quat-ri-èm'   Mum'sell' Fait - le - Poing.
O - der das Fräulein   ken - ne - kei - nen Scherz?

a punta
d'arco

гу - сель-цы = ба - ра-но-вы   стру - ноч-ки...   Тюкъ, тюкъ...
on chan-te doux, un'   jo-li - e   chan-son pour vous...   Tiouc, tiouc...
klin-ge Sai - te, kling. Laß uns ein   ar - tig Lie-del,   Pink, Pink,

430

*) come sopra

RENARD 119

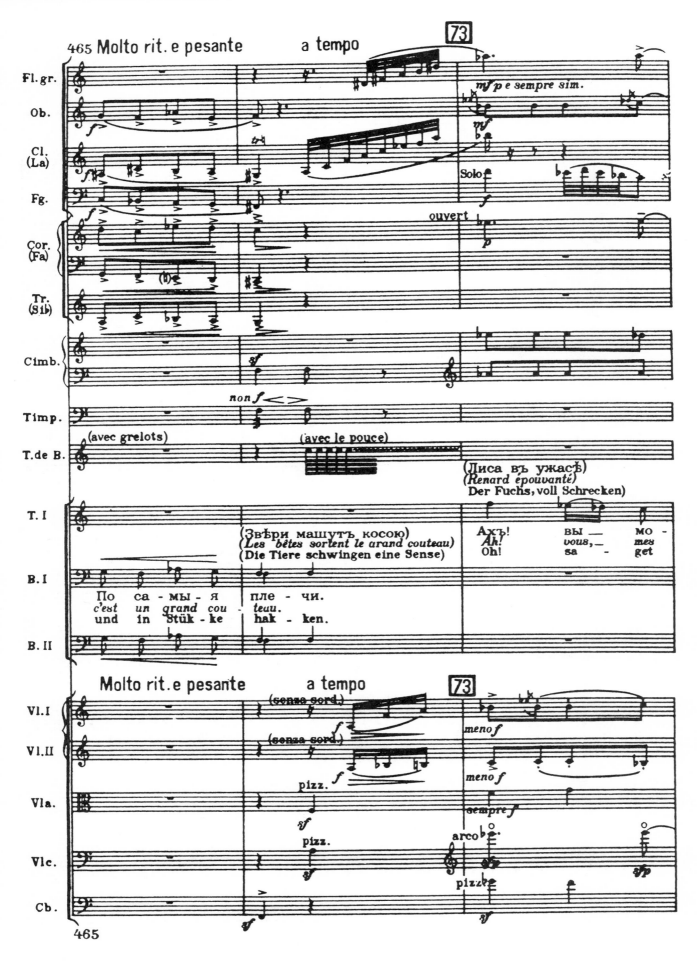

*) Переходъ звука „ѣ" въ звукъ „у" внезапенъ. Звукъ „у" слѣдуетъ произносить въ губы, подражая звуку низкой струны контрабаса.

*) какъ выше

préparez les baguettes en cuir.

-су зве́-ри хва-ти-ли,
bêt's t'ont at-tra-pée,
eh' du dich ver-se-hen,

-су зве́-ри хва-ти-ли, __ Да за-кам шили.
bêt's t'ont at-tra-pée, __ t'ont dé-chi rée.
eh' du dich ver-se-hen, __ um dich ge- sche-hen.

(Лиса свирѣпѣетъ и раз-
махиваетъ хвостомъ. Она
(1ый тенръ) кричитъ хво-
ту: „Ахъ! ты каналья,
такъ же тебя звѣри
ѣдятъ!"
(Звѣри хватаютъ лисій
хвостъ, выволакиваютъ
ее самою и душатъ ее)
(Renard pris de fureur, agite
la queue. Il crie en s'adressant
à celle-ci (I.er ténor): „Ah! canaille,
que les bêtes te mettent en mor-
ceaux!"
(Les bêtes attrapent la queue de
Renard, tirent Renard hors de
sa maison, et l'étranglent)
(Der Fuchs, von Wut erfaßt,
wedelt mit dem Schweif, er
schreit ihm zu) „Du Aas, wenn
die Viecher dich nur auffräßen!"
79 (Die Tiere fassen den Fuchs
beim Schweif, ziehen ihn
aus dem Hause heraus und
erwürgen ihn)

(Оба тенора и оба баса вопятъ благимъ матомъ) Лиса издыхаетъ
(*Les deux ténors et les deux basses hurlent de toutes leurs forces*) *Renard expire*
(Beide Tenöre und beide Bässe heulen mit voller Kraft.)Der Fuchs stirbt.

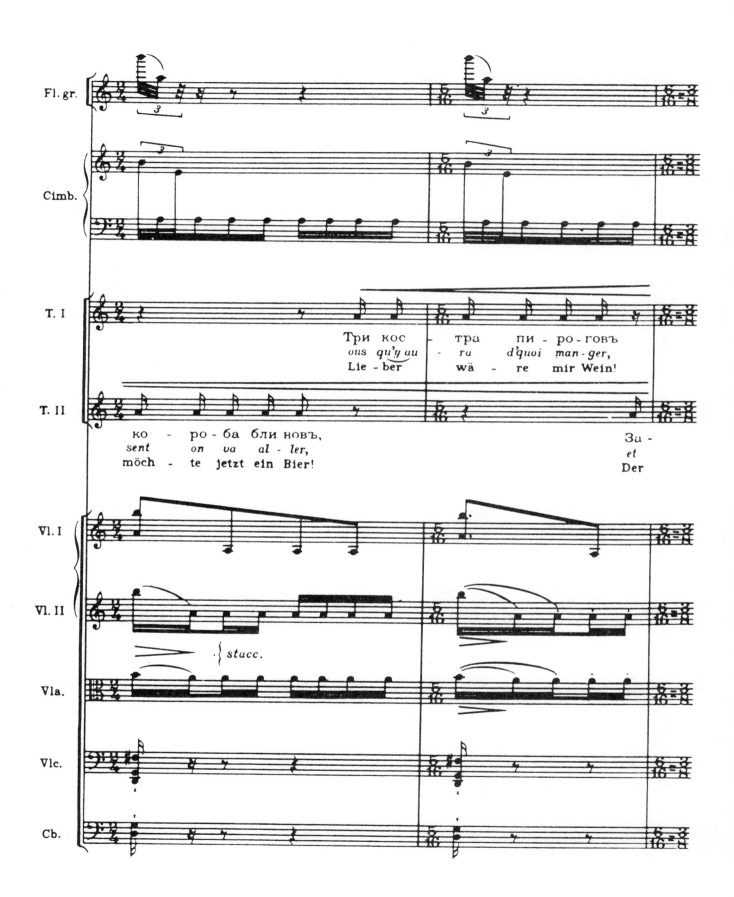

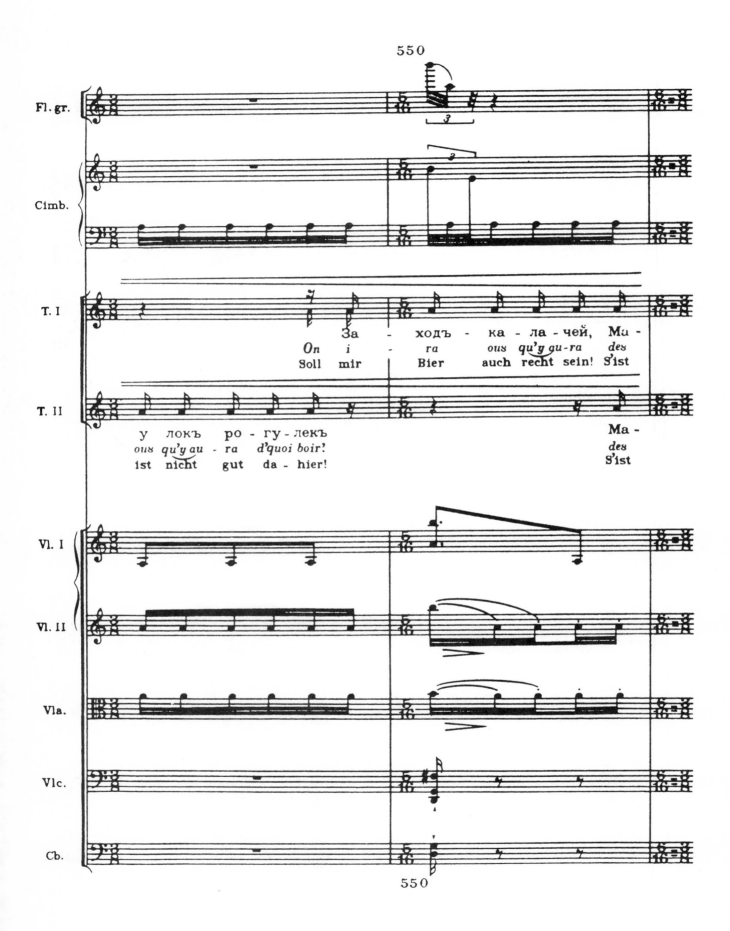

MARCHE [MARCH]

Departure of the Actors

153

HISTOIRE DU SOLDAT
[The Soldier's Tale, 1918]

To be read, played and sung
(in two parts)

For a reader and three actors
With small chamber ensemble

The composer's caricature of his collaborator. *Lausanne, 1917.*

Note

The beginning of 1918 was one of the darkest moments in Stravinsky's life. Although, like Diaghilev and many of the Russian intellectuals then living in Western Europe, he had felt exhilarated by the 1917 revolution, the Treaty of Brest-Litovsk sickened and humiliated him. He found himself completely cut off from his private resources in Russia; and for the first time the possibility must have occurred to him that he might never return to his native country. No new major work of his had been performed since 1914; and although both [*Renard*] and *The Wedding* were completed, it was clearly going to be impossible to produce them until after the war. He saw no immediate likelihood of help from Diaghilev, who was indeed at that moment in a position of great difficulty himself: so he decided—temporarily, at least—to break away from the Russian Ballet and do what he could to work out his own salvation.

One day, in the course of a discussion with Ramuz,[*] the idea came to him: 'Why not do something quite *simple*? Why not write together a piece that would need no vast theatre or large public; something with two or three characters and a handful of instrumentalists.' As no theatres were available, a special theatre would be improvised for the purpose, with scenery that could easily be set up in any hall or building, or even in the open air—in fact, a travelling theatre that would tour Switzerland and give performances in towns or even villages. But even so modest a plan needed financial backing; and it wasn't until Stravinsky had secured the patronage of Werner Reinhart of Winterthur that the collaborators were able to set to work.

As Ramuz was not a man of the theatre, he proposed to write a story which could be read, played and danced—in fact, a kind of mimed narration—while Stravinsky decided to compose a score that would be independent of the text and could be performed separately as a concert suite.

Next came the choice of subject. Stravinsky showed Ramuz [Afanasiev's] collection of Russian tales; and they were both struck by the cycle of legends dealing with the adventures of the soldier who deserts and the devil who carries off his soul. Although these refer particularly to the period of forced recruitment under Nicholas I, the collaborators decided to broaden and internationalise their treatment of the story—that is to say, in Ramuz's text the scene is laid in Switzerland (and it is open for English, German and other translators to vary the locality to suit their needs), and Stravinsky made his music as non-Russian as possible, even going so far as to use North and South American, Spanish and German material.

Ramuz confined the *dramatis personae* of *The Soldier's Tale* to four: the Soldier and the Devil (both speaking parts), the Princess (silent) and a Reader. In addition, the Princess and the Devil are required to dance. The Reader's role is particularly important and varied. Sometimes he is required to act as narrator; at others, to express the thoughts of the Soldier or address him direct; and also to comment generally on the action.

For the purpose of the plot, the Soldier's desertion is somewhat slurred over; but the fiddle he carries in his knapsack and which the Devil tries to win from him assumes a symbolic importance. In fact . . . the story becomes a kind of miniature version of the Faust legend. . . .

It was Stravinsky's part of the bargain that he should choose an extremely simple combination of instruments. In his *Chronicle*, he explains: 'The easiest solution would have been to use a polyphonic instrument like the piano or harmonium. The latter was out of the question, chiefly because of its dynamic poverty due to the complete absence of accents. Although the piano has much more varied polyphonic qualities and offers many particularly dynamic possibilities, I had to avoid it for two reasons: either my score would have seemed like a piano arrangement—and that would have given evidence of a certain lack of financial means, not at all in keeping with our intentions—or I should have had to use it as a solo instrument, exploiting every possibility of its technique. In other words, I should have had to be specially careful about the "pianism" of my score and make it into a vehicle of virtuosity in order to justify my choice. So there was nothing for it but to decide on a group of instruments, which could include the most representative types, in treble and bass, of the different instrumental families: for the strings, violin and double-bass; for the wood-wind, clarinet (because it has the biggest compass) and bassoon; for the brass, cornet and trombone; finally, the percussion to be played by a single musician; the whole, of course, under a conductor.' . . .

The percussion deserves special mention. On his return from America . . . , Ansermet had brought Stravinsky a selection of jazz material; and there is no doubt that this influenced him profoundly—(note, for instance, how closely the instrumentation of *The Soldier's Tale* resembles that of the 1916 New Orleans Dixieland jazzband° with its clarinet, trumpet, trombone, piano and drums)—so that he not only included a ragtime in his set of dances, but also built up his percussion on jazzband lines. . . .

After many delays and a prolonged period of rehearsal, the first performance took place at Lausanne on September 28, 1918. The scenery and costumes were by the Vaudois artist, René Auberjonois. Three students from Lausanne University played the roles of the Soldier, the Devil and the Reader; and Georges [Pitoëff] and his wife, [Loudmila,] came over from Geneva to dance the parts of the Devil and the Princess. Ansermet conducted; and the production was in the hands of Ramuz and Stravinsky.

FROM ERIC WALTER WHITE'S
Stravinsky: A Critical Survey°°

[°Charles-Ferdinand Ramuz. For a discussion of Stravinsky's earlier collaboration with this Swiss author, see p. 3 of this edition.]

°Probably refers to the 1918 recordings of the Original Dixieland Jazz Band.

°°Originally published by Philosophical Library, Inc., New York, 1948. Reprinted by Greenwood Press, London, 1979.

Histoire du Soldat: Scenario

The original publication of this score could only have presumed that the reader had a full script in hand in order to follow the complete story. Aside from scattered stage directions and a few passages of rhythmic speech within the set pieces, the score limited its storytelling to a succession of brief word cues, each introducing a new music section. All connective speeches, dialogues and descriptions of stage business—in other words, the heart of the tale—were omitted from the score.

The scenario that follows is meant to make up for these omissions, telling the complete tale of the Soldier and the Devil as a running narrative. The portions omitted from the original score publication appear in brackets. The division of the two acts into seven scenes (some sources say six), as well as the French title of each scene, follows the published program of *Histoire*'s first performance, in Lausanne, Switzerland, on 28 September 1918.

Part One. **Marche du Soldat** (The Soldier's March, pp. 163–168): Weary from his long walk home, the Soldier stops to rest.

"Scène au bord du ruisseau" (Scene One: "Beside a brook"). [The Soldier rummages through his knapsack, pulling out a religious medallion, some cartridges, an old mirror, his fiancée's picture, and, from the bottom, his fiddle.] Trying to tune it he laments, "It's too cheap to stay in tune."

Petits Airs au Bord du Ruisseau (Little Tunes Beside the Brook, pp. 169–172): As the Soldier plays, the Devil appears. [He is disguised as an old man carrying a butterfly net. The Devil offers to buy the fiddle but is turned down. Then he offers to swap his book for the fiddle—a magical book full of paper money, gold and a look into the future of the stock market! It's a deal! But finding he can't play the fiddle, the Devil invites the Soldier to his home, painting delicious images of luxury. The tempting invitation wipes away the Soldier's plans to see his mother and fiancée.

[The audience is assured that the Devil has kept his word. On the morning of the third day, the Devil (still in disguise) invites the Soldier (delighted with his visit) for a ride. Faster and faster goes the horse-drawn carriage until it takes to the air, flying high above the fields as the Devil repeatedly asks, "Have you any complaints?" Then, like magic, they're in the Soldier's home village.

[*"Scène du sac" (Scene Two: "The knapsack"/entering the village).* Reprise: **Marche du Soldat**. No one responds to the Soldier's cheery hellos, neither his neighbor in her garden nor his old friend the farmer. In the crowded village square the people seem afraid of him: door after door shuts in his face! What's this?! Even his mother screams and runs away. And his fiancée? Married! With two children! The Soldier suddenly grasps what's happened. He curses the Devil: it's not three days that have passed but three *years!* He is little more than a ghost among the living. The Soldier berates himself for his blindness, stupidity, self-indulgence . . . and for giving away his fiddle:] "And now, I ask you, what am I to do?"

Pastorale (pp. 173–174, until the fermata before Fig. 6): [The Devil appears disguised as a cattle merchant. The Soldier lunges at him with drawn saber, but his anger quickly dissolves into silent worry: what is he going to do now? The

Devil reminds him that the magic book is his key to great fortune—that, plus a proper soldierly attitude. (The Devil launches into a charade of military gestures to make his point.) But where is that book? The Soldier rumages in his knapsack. Out come the mirror, the medallion and, finally, the book. "But watch how you take care of it!" the Devil cautions. "It's worth millions!" The Devil takes the fiddle from his own pocket: "This is mine . . . that's yours . . . to each his own." He leads the Soldier away.] **Closing music** (p. 174, from Fig. 6 to the end).

[The book has worked wonders for the Soldier, accounting for more wealth than he can possibly use. To the accompaniment of drum rolls, the Reader recounts the Soldier's astounding successes as a merchant of any and all wares. But who needs wares to sell once one enters into the spirit of desire and possession? Why not have *everything* before one meets the finality of death?

[Yes, he has everything. And nothing. All that he has is as empty as a shell, false, dead and meaningless. Oh, to have what he once possessed in life—real things that count for something!: relaxing in the grass, delightful weekends, people watering their gardens, little girls playing . . . "Those people have nothing and everything. I have everything and nothing. Rich as I am, I'm a dead man among the living."°

[*"Scène du livre" (Scene Three: "The book"/ the Soldier seated at a desk in a room).* The book has failed him. It has no answers for his anguish. He throws it on the floor. The Devil appears as an old crone, peddling odds and ends. He offers to show his wares, exhibiting the Soldier's knapsack. "Look, sir," he implores, then, faster and faster, displays its contents: Watches? Necklaces? Some lace, perhaps? A silver medallion? No? A mirror, or a lovely framed portrait? (The Soldier shows some interest.) Or, perhaps, a little fiddle? The Soldier stands abruptly, moving quickly toward the Devil. "How much?" The Devil offers the fiddle. "Good friends always get along. Try it first before we talk price." The Soldier attempts to play but there is no sound. The Devil disappears.] The Soldier throws the fiddle with all his might.

Reprise: **Petits Airs au Bord du Ruisseau** (p. 175): He tears up the book in despair.

Part Two. Modified reprise: **Marche du Soldat** (pp. 176–180): Trudging along, wandering aimlessly, the Soldier no longer knows himself. [He only knows that he can't go on as before. He's thrown away his fine possessions. Now things seem to be as before—except, of course, for his missing sack and the precious things it held.

[*"Scène devant le rideau" (Scene Four: "In front of the curtain").* The Soldier finds himself in another country, enters a village inn and orders a drink. A sudden drumbeat jars him from his daydreaming. It is a public announcement that the King's only daughter lies ill in bed, neither sleeping nor eating nor speaking. But (the King proclaims) his daughter shall wed the man who heals her! A former soldier approaches: "What have you got to lose? Give it a try! Just tell them you're an army doctor!"] "Why not?" says the Soldier, banging his fist on the table. He sets off to the palace.

Marche Royale (Royal March, pp. 181–191): During the music the curtain rises, then soon falls, on a room in the

---

°In a later Chester edition of the score, this reverie is accompanied by a reprise of the "Petits Airs," the same music that serves the next scene in all editions.

palace. The Devil is disguised as a violinist, dressed in the height of fashion.

["*Scène du jeu de cartes*" (Scene Five: "The card game" / *a dimly lit room in the palace*). The Soldier must wait a day to see the Princess. Seated at a table with a pack of cards, he daydreams about a possible turn of fortune. But the Devil appears, holding the fiddle, taunting him for his great misfortune, belittling his chance to find happiness. It is the Devil who will cure the Princess!

[The Reader challenges the Soldier to play cards with the Devil. "He's got you because you have his money. Get rid of it all and you're saved! Play cards with him; he's going to win." The Devil is astonished at the Soldier's offer, but eagerly agrees as the Soldier empties his pockets. The Devil (with the fiddle resting across his knees) wins hand after hand, gleefully taunting the Soldier: "You'll go hungry, barefoot, naked! You see? Total defeat!" But the Soldier doubles his bet, then stakes everything, every penny!

[The Devil is overcome with victory. The Solder forces a drink on him, then refills the glass again and again. The Devil collapses but the Soldier, flush with new-found freedom, pours drink after drink down the Devil's throat until his victim is senseless.] At the Reader's urging to "take back your own," the Soldier grabs the fiddle and begins to play.

Petit Concert (Little Concert, pp. 192–200): During the music, at Fig. 22, the lights come up as the Princess is assured that her savior is on his way. "He can do anything because he's found himself again! Just as he's come back from the dead, he will bring you back to life as well!"

["*Scène de la fille guérie*" (Scene Six: "The cured maiden" / *in the Princess's room*). The Princess, immobile, lies on her bed. The Soldier enters and begins to play his fiddle.]

Trois Danses (Three Dances, pp. 201–212, played without pause): **Tango** (p. 201), **Valse** (Waltz, p. 204), **Ragtime** (p. 208): The Princess rises and begins to dance.

[The Princess has just fallen into the Soldier's arms when horrible shrieks announce the entrance of the Devil (no longer in disguise), who crawls onstage. He circles about the Soldier, first begging for the fiddle, then trying to snatch it away. The Princess takes refuge behind the Soldier as the Devil moves about faster and faster. The Soldier has an idea: he begins to play the fiddle.]

Danse du Diable (The Devil's Dance, pp. 213–217): [The Devil is beset by contortions! He can't stand still!] The Soldier and the Princess drag the Devil away, then return to embrace.

Petit Choral (Little Chorale, p. 218), then, without pause, **Couplet du Diable** (The Devil's Song, pp. 218–220): The Devil reappears to issue a bitter warning: the game's not over yet! He vanishes as the young couple continue their embrace.

Grand Choral (Great Chorale, pp. 221–222): At each pause, the Reader declaims a small portion of his final speech. [Before Fig. 1]: "Don't be tempted to add what you now have to what you once had. You can't mix up what you are with what you were." [Before Fig. 2]: "You must learn to choose. You can't have everything." [Before Fig. 3]: "A single happiness is *all* happiness. But two? It's as though neither existed." [Just after Fig. 4]: " 'I have everything,' he thinks. But one day she says, 'I know almost nothing about you.' " [At the last pause]: " 'It all goes back a long time, when I was a soldier, at home with my mother in the village. It's so far away that I've forgotten where it is.' "

[The Soldier longs to return home. "We'd be back before you know it. No one will be the wiser. Perhaps this time my mother will know me and she can come live with us. Then I'll have everything." He hesitates but the Princess encourages him. (The Devil crosses in front of the curtain, dressed in a splendid scarlet costume.) The couple are on their way, now almost at the village. The Soldier has gone ahead; the Princess is a bit behind. (The Devil crosses once more.)

["*Scène des limites franchies*" (Scene Seven: "An overdrawn account" / *reentering the village*). The Soldier turns, calls out to the Princess, gesturing. Going on, he reaches the edge of the village as the Devil appears in front of him, once more holding the fiddle. The Devil begins to play.]

Marche Triomphale du Diable (Triumphal March of the Devil, pp. 223–230): [Unresisting, the Soldier follows the Devil. He hesitates as a voice calls out to him from afar, but the Devil beckons him. The two leave the scene as the voice calls one last time.]

ENGLISH NARRATIVE BY RONALD HERDER,
BASED ON A FRENCH LIBRETTO BY C. F. RAMUZ

Instrumentation

Clarinet in A, B♭ [Clarinetto, Cl. (La, Si♭)]
Bassoon [Fagotto, Fg.]

Cornet in A, B♭ [Cornet à pistons, C. à P., Pist, (La, Si♭)]
Trombone (Tenor-Bass) [Trombone (Ten.-Bas.), Trb.]

Violin [Violino, Vl.]
Bass [Contrabasso, C. B.]

Percussion [Batterie, Batt.] (*one player*):°
    Triangle [Triangle, Trgl.]
    Cymbals (*pair*) [Piatti]
    Cymbal attached to Bass Drum [Cymb(ale) fixée à la Gr. C.]
    Tambourine [Tamb(our) de Basque, T(mb). de B., T.d.b.]
    2 Side (Snare) Drums—one large, one small—with snares off [Caisse claire sans
        timbre—grande taille, petite taille; Caisse cl.; C. cl.; C. cl. s. t. gr. t.]
    Field Drum (or Large Snare) with snare release [Tambour sans timbre: Tmb.
        s. timbre, T.s.t.; Tambour à timbre: Tmb. à t., T. à t.]
    Bass Drum [Grosse Caisse, Gr. C., G. C.]

(For a list of percussion beaters, see the Glossary, p. v, under *baguette*.)

°The original score diagrammed a simple disposition of the percussion instruments to facilitate performance by one player. The score, however, contains explicit instructions along the same lines, particularly for more complex passages.

PART ONE
MARCHE DU SOLDAT (AIRS DE MARCHE)
[The Soldier's March (Marching Tunes)]

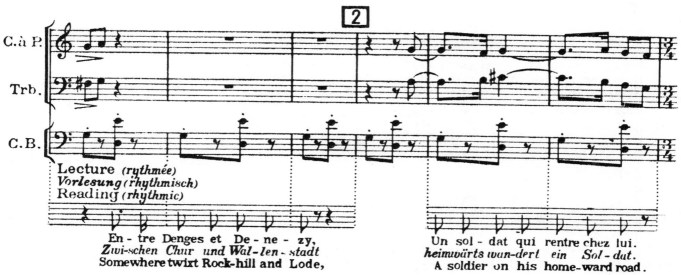

marche de - puis   long temps dé - jà.
wan-dert was   er wan-dern mag.
And   he's tramp'd from morn till eve.

Tamb. de Basque
Caisse claire sans timbre, grande taille
Grosse Caisse

A mar-ché, a beau-coup marché,
Ur-laub hat er gan-ze vierzehn Tag.
Still must trudge, tramp and trudge and roam,

*) Tenir dans la main droite une baguette en jonc à tête en capoc et se servir de celle-ci pour frapper le tambour de basque et la caisse claire; dans la main gauche - la mailloche pour frapper la grosse caisse

*)Pour les baguettes et leur distribution comme ci-dessus

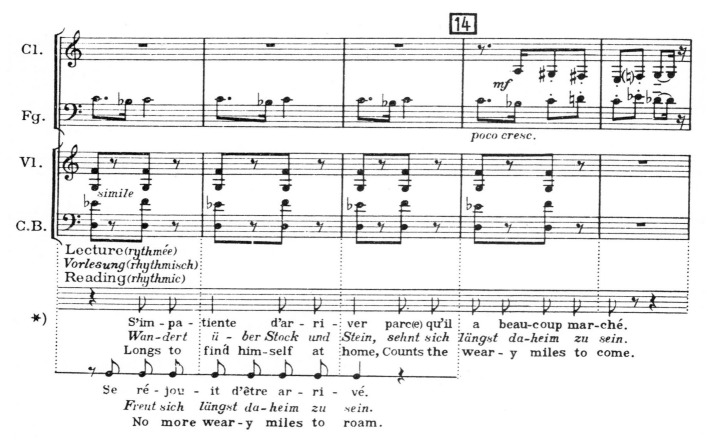

S'im - pa - tiente d'ar - ri - ver parc(e) qu'il a beau-coup mar-ché.
Wan - dert ü - ber Stock und Stein, sehnt sich längst da-heim zu sein.
Longs to find him-self at home, Counts the wear - y miles to come.

Se ré - jou - it d'être ar - ri - vé.
Freut sich längst da-heim zu sein.
No more wear-y miles to roam.

Le soldat s'arrête
Der Soldat steht still
The soldier stops

Le rideau se lève. La musique (Batterie) continue. Le décor représente les bords d'un ruisseau. Le soldat entre en scène.
Der Vorhang öffnet sich. Andauernde Musik (Schlagwerk). Die Szenerie gibt das Ufer eines Baches wieder. Der Soldat tritt auf.
The curtain rises. The music (Batterie) continues. The scene shows the banks of a stream. Enter the Soldier.

*) Pour la reprise de la Marche pendant la lecture qui précède la 2ème scène
Bei der Wiederholung des Marsches vor der 2. Szene
For the repetition of the March during the reading which precedes Scene II

PETITS AIRS AU BORD DU RUISSEAU
[Little Tunes Beside the Brook]
(Music for Scene One)

Le soldat, accordant le violon:"On voit que c'est du bon marché il faut tout le temps l'accorder".…
Der Soldat, die Geige stimmend: „Wertlose War, die niemand nimmt. Die Geige ist total verstimmt!"
The soldier, tuning the fiddle: „'Tis a cheap and gimcrack thing, and out of tune in every string".…

Le diable se cache
Der Teufel versteckt sich
The Devil hides himself

PASTORALE

(Music for [the end of] Scene Two)

La musique commence immédiatement après la phrase de la lecture: Et à présent qu'est-ce que je vais faire? répétée pour 3ème fois

Die Musik beginnt unmittelbar nach der 3. Wiederholung der Worte: „Was soll ich jetzt tun?"

The music begins immediately after the sentence in the reading: "And now I ask you, what am I to do?" (repeated twice)

Musique de la fin de la 2ème Scène
Schlußmusik der 2. Szene
Music for the close of Scene II

Le rideau se baisse
Der Vorhang fällt
The curtain falls

PETITS AIRS AU BORD DU RUISSEAU
[*Reprise*: Little Tunes Beside the Brook]
(*Music for [the end of] Scene Three*)

Le Soldat jette de toutes ses forces le violon dans la coulisse, puis:
Der Soldat schmeißt die Geige in die Kulisse, hierauf:
The Soldier throws the fiddle with all his might into the wings, then:

Le soldat déchire le livre
Der Soldat zerreißt das Buch
The Soldier tears the book into pieces

Le rideau tombe
Der Vorhang fällt
Curtain falls

PART TWO
MARCHE DU SOLDAT (AIRS DE MARCHE)
[*Reprise (modified)*: The Soldier's March (Marching Tunes)]

*)**M.dr.** = bagu.en jonc à tète en capoc pour le Tmb.de B.et le Tmb.s.timbre
 M. g. = mailloche pour la G.C.

Lecture (rythmée):
Vorlesung (rhythmisch):
Reading (rhythmic):

En - tre Denges et De - ne - zy,   et il s'en va droit de-vant lui
Zwi - schen Chur und Wal - len-stadt   wan-dert wei - ter der Sol - dat.
Some-where twixt Rock-hill and Lode   Tramp-ing straight a - long the road.

Où est-ce qu'il va comme ça, marche) de-puis long temps dé - jà.
Wan-dert, wan-dert, steht nicht still, *kei - ner weiß, wo - hin er will.*
Where's he go - ing? Who can say? Walk-ing trud-ging all the day.

Le ruis - seau, en-suite le pont, où est-ce qu'il va?
Über Bach und Brük-ken-bo-gen ist er wan-dernd
Past the brook and bridge he goes. Where's he off to?

le sait-on?
hin-ge-zogen.
No one knows.

Le lecteur continue ...... Il ne le sait pas lui même ....etc.
....jusqu'à: avec le sac en moins et les choses dedans.

Der Vorleser fährt fort...... Ein kurzes Glück ....etc.
....bis: man hat den Sack — doch der ist leer. | La Musique de la Marche reprend.
Wiederholung des Marsches.
The reader continues from ...... He does not know himself ....etc. | Repetition of the March
....until: minus the sack and all it bore.

Et   le dos tour - né au pays
Geht, den Rücken   ab - gekehrt,
Now his back is   turned to Lode

A   é - té,
weiter, weiter
Still he tramps,

a en-core   é - té   a mar-ché,   a beaucoup marché.
sei-nen Weg ü - ber Stock und Stein und Steg. Trudges on all day.
still he tramps trudges all the day.

MARCHE ROYALE
[Royal March]

Lecteur: *Nouveau coup de poing:„ou je vais? je vais chez le Roi!"*
Vorleser: *„Zum König! Könnt Ihr denn noch fragen?"*
Reader: *New blows with the fist: "Where am I going? Going to see the King!"*

*) au bord et au milieu de la membrane, comme plus haut.

On voit une chambre du palais. Le diable en tenue de violoniste mondain.
Man sieht einen Saal im Palast. Der Teufel steht als Geigenvirtuose verkleidet da.
One sees a room in a palace. The Devil is there dressed as a Virtuoso Violinist

Le Soldat: Ah! c'est comme ça, Eh bien, tiens!... tiens... tiens...
Le Lecteur: Tu reprends ton bien.
Der Soldat: In die Gurgel diesen Resten
Der Vorleser: Wer zuletzt lacht, lacht am besten
The Soldier: That's right. There...'tis down
The Reader: ...take back your own

PETIT CONCERT
[Little Concert]

*) Comme plus haut, au bord et au milieu de la membrane (bag. à tête en capoc)

Lecture: Mademoiselle, à présent on peut
le dire...
Vorlesung: Mein Fräulein mit dem Honigmund
Reading: Princess, you now may be quite
reassured...

TROIS DANSES [Three Dances]
Tango

Clarinetto in La

Violino

Caisse claire sans timbre grande taille

Grosse Caisse

une Cymbale fixée à la Gr. C.

*) Remarque générale pour la percussion du TANGO

L'exécutant tient la mailloche (de la Gr. C.) dans sa main gauche et dans sa main droite une baguette à tête de capoc (avec le manche en jonc). Les notes avec les queues en haut appartiennent à la main droite (c. à. d. à la baguette en capoc), celles avec les queues en bas, à la main gauche, (c. à. d. à la mailloche). La cymbale (fixée à la Gr. C.) est légèrement frappée au bord, seulement par le manche en jonc de la baguette en capoc. Pour la disposition des tambours consultez la **page consacrée à la dis-position de l'orchestre.**

La princesse se lève du lit
Die Prinzessin erhebt sich vom Lager
The Princess rises from her couch

Elle danse
Sie tanzt
She begins to dance

* Glissez avec l'archet de toute sa longueur jusqu'au signe ⊠
Sur la corde Ré jusqu'au même signe ⊠

* Exception faite des endroits marqués par le „saltando"

Valse [Waltz]

Ragtime

*) Toute cette percussion est (légèrement) frappée avec la tringle du triangle. Le triangle est tenu de la main gauche de l'exécutant; à sa droite, se trouvent (très prés) l'un en face de l'autre, la C. cl. et le Tamb. de basque (posés de champ, ce qui est plus commode pour l'exécutant); à sa gauche la Grosse caisse.

*) La Gr. C. se trouve à gauche et les 2 C. cl. juste en face de l'exécutant, et très près l'une de l'autre. Frappez ces instruments avec une baguette à tête en capoc que l'exécutant tient dans sa main gauche. Dans sa main droite il tient une baguette mince à petite tête en éponge. (qu'il lui faudrait tenir prête pour le No 34)

**) Exécuter avec la bag. à tête d'éponge dont l'exécutant prendra soin de tenir la tête tournée en bas et de la manier rien qu' avec les doigts (le bras restant parfaitement immobile) de façon à donner au rythme une allure mécanique et précise

Le rideau se baisse et se lève de nouveau
Der Vorhang fällt und hebt sich wieder
The Curtain falls and then rises again

DANSE DU DIABLE
[The Devil's Dance]

*) Placez ces deux instruments de champ, très prés l'un de l'autre de façon à pouvoir manier aisément la baguette (m. dr.) entre leurs membranes dans le mouvement indiqué.

Après cette danse où le Diable épuisé tombe à terre sur un signe du Soldat, la Princesse prend le Diable par une patte et à eux deux ils le traînent dans la coulisse. Ils reviennent au milieu de la scène et tombent dans les bras l'un de l'autre sous les sons du „Petit Choral" qui suit.

Mit Schluß des Tanzes fällt der Teufel erschöpft zu Boden. Der Soldat nimmt die Prinzessin bei der Hand. Man sieht, daß sie keine Furcht mehr hat. Dann, auf ein Zeichen des Soldaten, packt sie den Teufel bei einer seiner Tatzen, und zu zweien schleifen sie ihn hinter die Kulisse. Sie kommen wieder und fallen sich inmitten der Bühne in die Arme. Einsatz des kleinen Chorals.

At the end of this dance, when the Devil falls down exhausted, at a sign from the Soldier the Princess takes the Devil by one paw, and between them they drag him off the stage. They return, take up their position in the centre of the stage and fall into each other's arms to the strains of the "Little Choral" which follows.

PETIT CHORAL [Little Chorale]

Embrassement / *Umarmung* / the embrace

COUPLET DU DIABLE [The Devil's Song]

Le Diable disparaît. Le Soldat et la princesse se tiennent toujours embrassés
Der Teufel verschwindet. Soldat und Prinzessin halten sich noch immer umschlungen
The Devil disappears. The Soldier and the Princess are still embraced

GRAND CHORAL [Great Chorale]

Note: Les parties lues sont intercalées entre les reprises du Choral
Die Vorlesung wird durch Wiederholungen des Chorals unterbrochen
The reading is interrupted by repetitions of the Choral

„*Man soll zu dem, was man besitzt, nicht das Besessne fügen wollen.*"

Un bonheur est tout le bonheur; deux, c'est comme s'ils n'existaient plus

„*Drum sei der Augenblick genützt. Das größte Glück gerät ins Rollen*"

But one joy at a time; two cancel one another

"Rufst du ein zweites dir herzu, verlassen beide dich im Nu"

raconte moi, raconte moi un peu de toi
"Nun hab' ich alles... von deiner Seele!"
About your past, I'd like to hear

sul Ré

loin, bien loin, et j'ai oublié le chemin
"Es war einmal... geblieben sein?"
Mother dwelt in a villagecot, the road to which I've quite forgot

MARCHE TRIOMPHALE DU DIABLE

[Triumphal March of the Devil]

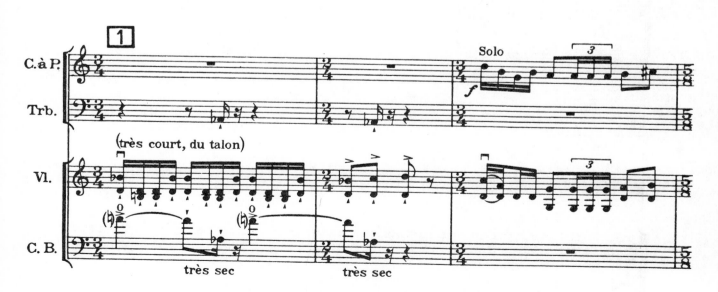

Le rideau tombe lentement
Der Vorhang fällt langsam
The curtain falls slowly

END OF EDITION